UK GARAGE IS A DANCE MUSIC GENRE THAT EMERGED IN THE MID 90'S AROUND THE LONDON NIGHTCLUB & PIRATE RADIO CIRCUIT.

HEAVILY INSPIRED BY THE GARAGE HOUSE SOUND, WHICH ORIGINATED IN THE STATES. PRODUCERS FUSED HOUSE MUSIC GROOVES WITH ELEMENTS OF R&B & JUNGLE WHICH WERE HUGE AT THE TIME IN THE UK.

IT WAS A GENRE THAT TOOK THE COUNTRY BY STORM, AND SPAWNED OTHER POPULAR GENRES SUCH AS GRIME, DUBSTEP, BASSLINE.

THIS BOOK SHINES LIGHT ON LOADS OF THE VITAL UK GARAGE LABELS, SOME OF THE HEAVY HITTING NEW COMERS, A FEW CHART TOPPERS, WHILE ALSO CELEBRATING LABELS THAT HAVE SINCE BECOME DORMANT OR SHUT THE DOOR...

Words
Chris Dexta &
Alex Chapman (Immerse)

Editor
Colin Steven

Design
Banana Gun

Publishers
Southside Circulars
& Velocity Press

Originally Printed
June 2022

Revised Edition
May 2023

southsidecirculars.com
velocitypress.uk

VP024

ISBN: 978-1-913231-41-5

THE ICON CATALOGUE
UK GARAGE
VOL. 1

01. 4 LIBERTY RECORDS
02. ABSOLUTE CORRUPTION
03. ALL GOOD RECORDS
04. BINGO BEATS
05. BOOBY TRAP
06. CASA TRAX
07. DANGEROUS DUBZ
08. DANSU DISCS
09. DAT PRESSURE RECORDS
10. DR BANANA
11. FIRST CLASS
12. GROOVE YARD
13. ICE CREAM
14. JONNY BISCUIT RECORDS
15. KMA PRODUCTIONS
16. LOCKED ON
17. LOVE PEACE & UNITY
18. MANCHU
19. MOODSWING
20. NEW YORK SOUNDCLASH
21. OBSTACLE RECORDS
22. OUTLAW
23. PAPER MONEY
24. PHONE TRAXXX
25. PROLIFIC
26. PUBLIC DEMAND
27. RED ROSE RECORDINGS
28. RHYTHM DIVISION
29. SOCIAL CIRCLES
30. SOLO RECORDINGS
31. SOUND OF UNDERGROUND LDN
32. STRICTLY UNDERGROUND
33. SWING CITY
34. THIRST RECORDINGS
35. TIME 2 FLEX
36. TIME IS NOW
37. UNDA VYBE
38. VERY IMPORTANT PLASTIC
39. VIBESEY
40. VITAL ESSENCE

4 LIBERTY

1993 - 2002

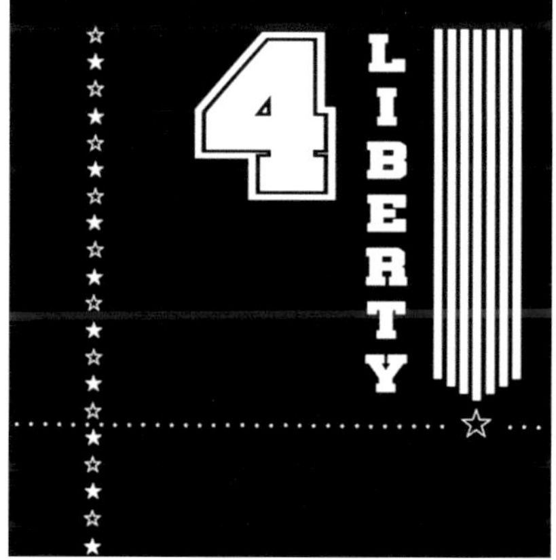

Tony Portelli's 4 Liberty & 4 Liberty Ltd churned out some killer cuts. From the beautiful Deep House grooves of the labels first release in 1993, they represented the full spectrum of House & Garage sounds.

THE ESSENTIALS

DREEM TEEM 'THE THEME'

'LIFT ME UP (GROOVE CHRONICLES REMIX)'

ABSOLUTE CORRUPTION

1998 - 2000

Public Demand's offshoot label Absolute Corruption may only have 7 releases, but when the first release (Steve Gurley's mix of "Goodbye") landed, you knew this label was going to go down in history!

THE ESSENTIALS

N.C.A. 'GOODBYE'

ANTHONEY 'IN THE HOUSE (NEW HORIZONS MIXES)'

ALL GOOD

1998 - 2002

All Good Records has got that unmistakeably 'London' 2-Step sound. Unsurprising, since it burst out of South East London in 1998 with a 12-inch from Cisko & label co-owner Dave 'All Good' H!

THE ESSENTIALS

CISKO 'DREAMER'

SOVEREIGN 'ONE ON ONE'

BINGO BEATS

2000 - 2009

DJ Zinc's label - started after the success of '138 Trek' as a home for his Breakbeat Garage tracks, featuring music & remixes from Wookie, Zed Bias, Menta & early Chase & Status tunes. Went full-on D&B from 2005.

THE ESSENTIALS

JAMMIN 'HOLD ON'
JAMMIN 'KINDA FUNKY'

BOOBY TRAP

1997 - 2000

Owned & run by the D.E.A. Project (Dub Enforcement Agents). Originally a Hardcore / Jungle label - 'Booby Trap' switched to putting out purely UKG from 1997 releasing music from the group and their many aliases.

THE ESSENTIALS

D.E.A. PROJECT 'MARIAH'

DJ PARA 'CALL ME'

CASA TRAX

1995 - 2000

Casa Trax were responsible for putting out some seminal UK garage records. Tracks like Tuff Jam's 'Experience' and 'History of House Music' are true classics of the genre. Essential listening for any UKG head!

THE ESSENTIALS

DUB SYNDICATE 'I NEED YOUR LOVE 99'

TUFF JAM EXPERIENCE 'EXPERIENCE'

DANGEROUS DUBZ

1997

Very short lived sister label of 'DUBZ FOR KLUBZ' - started as a platform to house collaborations between Paul Benjamin & Jeremy Sylvester.

THE ESSENTIALS

UNKNOWN 'DON'T HOLD BACK'
UNKNOWN 'YOU WON'T GET AWAY'

DANSU DISCS

2017 - PRESENT

DANSU DISCS

Manchester based label showcasing UK Garage, House, Techno, and everything in between. Some of the scene's leading lights have released on the label in the past few years.

THE ESSENTIALS

INTEPLANETARY CRIMINAL 'CONFUSED EP'

BAILEY IBBS 'GURL EP'

DAT PRESSURE

1997 - PRESENT

DAT PRESSURE RECORDS

Groove Chronicles are responsible for all manner of classic remixes & productions, also responsible for Dat Pressure Records. Pirate radio anthems, vocals, 2-Step, 4x4 - it's all there in the back catalogue.

THE ESSENTIALS

GROOVE CHRONICLES '99'

STERLING STYLES 'NOBODY BUT YOU'

DR BANANA

2016 - PRESENT

Dr.Banana started as a label for new music, but found success in reissuing lost cuts from back in the day, and has since become a lifestyle brand, with limited edition garms and vinyl only releases.

THE ESSENTIALS

DJ DELLER 'ROMANTIC CALL 2001'

DJ BACKSPIN 'WEAPON '97'

FIRST CLASS

1998 - 2001

UK Garage royalty Chris Mack owned label alongside Old Soul & Suspect Recordings - showcasing his own productions. Expect to be parting with some serious cash if you want to own them all!

THE ESSENTIALS

CHRIS MACK 'KA-BOOM EP'

CHRIS MACK 'EP VOLUME 3'

GROOVE YARD

1995 - 1999

Label from DJ Einstein, launched with a sample laden Garage House 4-tracker. He never looked back, with the following years seeing all manner of sub labels & bumping cuts coming out of the Groove Yard!

THE ESSENTIALS

KALANI BOB & REMEGEL 'THE CHEESE & PICKLE EP'

EINSTEIN & CHEWY 'KUTZ FROM THE LAB VOL 1'

ICE CREAM

1995 - PRESENT

Set up by Tim Deluxe, Omar Adimora (10° Below) & Boogie Beat Records' Andy Lysandrou. Early releases were bumpy Garage House tracks by RIP Productions. An all time great UKG label!

THE ESSENTIALS

DOUBLE 99 'RIPGROOVE'

R.I.P. 'DEEP DUBS VOLUME 1'

JONNY BISCUIT RECORDS

1997 - 2001

Not many UKG tunes have had as much playtime as 'Lost in Vegas' - but there's plenty more in the bag to get your teeth into. If you're wondering who 'Jonny Biscuit' is - it's none other than Jungle legend Dr. S. Gachet!

THE ESSENTIALS

ROCSTEADY PRESENTS MOVIN' U 'WHATCHA GONNA DO'
SOME TREAT 'LOST IN VEGAS'

KMA PRODUCTIONS

1997 - 1998

Only two releases but boy are they weighty! Both by Ian & Rodney Degale, better known as KMA. The 'Breakin Out EP' combines influences from UKG, Jungle & Breaks, and 'The Fear Returns' is a heavyweight dancefloor smasher.

THE ESSENTIALS

KMA 'KAOTIC MADNESS'

KMA 'CAPE FEAR'

LOCKED ON

1997 - PRESENT

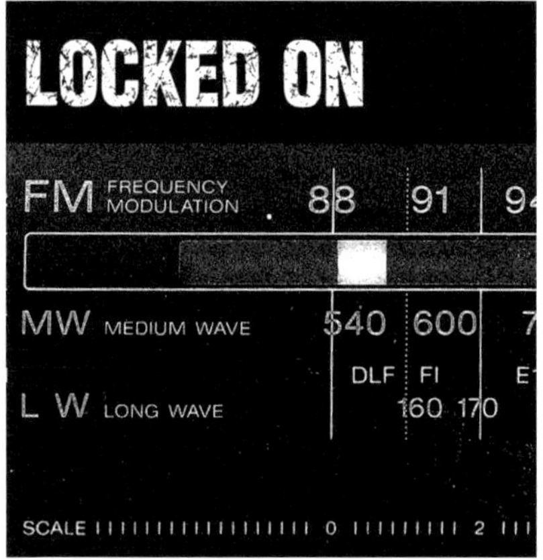

Launched by Tarik Nashnush out of the Pure Groove record shop. Loads of compilations focusing on the London pirate radio sound. Later achieved big crossover success with The Streets, Artful Dodger & Zed Bias!

THE ESSENTIALS

NU BIRTH 'ANYTIME'

US ALLIANCE 'ALL I KNOW'

LOVE PEACE & UNITY

1997 - 2006

Discogs 'wantlists' all over the world are peppered with Love Peace & Unity cuts. Some of the rarest and most sought after vinyl in the scene were put out on this label. Worth every penny of your hard earned cash!

THE ESSENTIALS

ANTHILL MOB 'ENCHANTED RHYTHMS'

MYSTIC MATT & THE ANTHILL MOB 'BURNIN'

MANCHU

1999 - 2004

MANCHU
recordings

Wookie launched Manchu Recordings with the monster 12 inch 'Down On Me / Scrappy' in 1999. Wookie's darker, breakbeat tinged UKG sound took dancefloors by storm in the late 90's and early 00's.

THE ESSENTIALS

WOOKIE 'DOWN ON ME / SCRAPPY'

EXEMEN 'FAR EAST / DUPPY'

MOODSWING

2019 - PRESENT

Perception has a reputation as being one of the best UKG DJs around, due to his dubplate filled sets. He launched the label in 2019 with his own 'Isla EP', 4 fresh sounding cuts, with a nod to UKG's 90's roots.

THE ESSENTIALS

DJ PERCEPTION 'ISLA EP'

SKY JOOSE 'THE RETURN OF SKY JOOSE'

NEW YORK SOUNDCLASH

1994 - PRESENT

Despite the name, N.Y.S. is a UK based label formed by Dem 2, a home for their house & garage productions. Recently, founding member Dean Boylan has released a string of new & old productions - sounding better than ever!

THE ESSENTIALS

TUFF JAM 'TUFF JAMS VOL.1'
DEM 2 'DA BUD SESSIONS VOL.1'

OBSTACLE

2015 - 2019

Run from Berlin, Germany - Obstacle Records put out 3 solid EPs, paying homage to the sounds of legendary UK labels like Locked On & Nice'n'Ripe, with a fresh interpretation of those classic UK Garage origins.

THE ESSENTIALS

LESUS 'THE BELL EP'

MOODSWING 'OUTBREAK EP'

OUTLAW

1997 - 1999

OUTLAW RECORDS

This short lived UKG imprint was home to some of the scene's most wanted records! Original tunes & remixes from the likes of Masterstepz, Groove Chronicles, Steve Gurley, Artful Dodger, Operator & many others.

THE ESSENTIALS

MASTERSTEPZ 'MELODY'

OPERATOR & BAFFLED 'THINGS ARE NEVER'

PAPER MONEY

2000 - 2001

One of the in house labels from the So Solid Crew, home to all of their big hits as well as some of the lesser known underground cuts made by the extended So Solid family...

THE ESSENTIALS

SO SOLID CREW 'OH NO!'

SO SOLID CREW 'DILEMMA'

PHONE TRAXXX

2018 - 2021

The origins of the label remain a mystery, contactable only via telephone! We do know that it was a 5 part vinyl only series. Making use of vintage mobile phones, an SMS hotline & unmistakeably bumpy basslines...

THE ESSENTIALS

PHONE TRAXX 'VOLUME 1'

PHONE TRAXX 'VOLUME 2'

PROLIFIC

1998 - 2013

Label from none other than the legendary MJ Cole, who wasted no time in putting out the type of beautifully crafted, melodic garage sounds that made him so well known. Relaunched in 2004 after a 6 year break.

THE ESSENTIALS

BOX CLEVER 'TALK TO ME'

MJ COLE 'TALKBOX'

PUBLIC DEMAND

1994 - 2014

Heavyweight label which has been cemented into the genre's DNA. Releasing a string of vocal chart tracks in the late. Releases from Artful Dodger, Dub Conspiracy, Dreem Team, Wideboys, Sticky, the list goes on..

THE ESSENTIALS

'SPIRIT OF THE SUN (STEVE GURLEY REMIX)'
MANHATTAN BROOKLYN 'JOIN HANDS'

RED ROSE

1998 - 2002

Started by Ian Hughes (Oracles) & Tony Wybrow, Red Rose are responsible for breaking DJ Luck & MC Neat, and responsible for the success of the hit tack 'Something In Your Eyes' by Ed Case.

THE ESSENTIALS

TROUBLESOME 'TROUBLESOME'

ED CASE 'SOMETHING IN YOUR EYES'

RHYTHM DIVISION

1996 - 2009

The label of the much loved (and missed) Rhythm Division record shop in Bow, East London. The early EPs are changing hands for several hundred pounds and when you hear them you'll know why! Killer cuts all day!

THE ESSENTIALS

VARIOUS 'THE SUNDAY KLUBB EP VOLUME 3'

TWO AS ONE & MJ COLE 'BODY HEAT'

SOCIAL CIRCLES

1997 - 2004

Founded by Jason Kaye. Many classic sought after records in the catalogue. Responsible for huge hits by Ms Dynamite & Sticky, as well as cuts from Ordinary People, Zed Bias, The Wideboys, Donaeo and many more.

THE ESSENTIALS

ORDINARY PEOPLE 'BABY YOU MAKE MY HEART SING'

E.S. DUBS 'STANDARD HOODLUM ISSUE'

SOLO RECORDINGS

2000 - 2017

Label founded by Matt 'Jam' Lamont - features reissues of some huge UKG classics (does it get any bigger than 'Feel My Love'?), loads of new bits & remixes as well. Expect plenty shuffles and swinging grooves.

THE ESSENTIALS

DRAMA 'KEEPER OF THE KEYS EP'

ARTIFACT 'FROM RUSSIA WITH DUBS VOL.2'

SOUND OF UNDERGROUND LONDON

1997 - 2003

Exactly what it says on the tin - The sound of underground London! Bumping underground UKG cuts, instant classics as soon as the first release hit the shelves in 1997.

THE ESSENTIALS

UNDERGROUND SOLUTION 'GET HAPPY / UNDERGROUND'
SOLUTION 'US DUB EXPERIENCE EP'

STRICTLY UNDERGROUND

1988 - 2008

Label started by Mark 'Ruff' Ryder, releasing Hardcore / Jungle & UKG. The UKG period was all Mark's own music under various aliases - some going for big boss level monies! Also home to anthem tracks by MCs Vapour & Special.

THE ESSENTIALS

DJ DUBZ 'SCREAM'

MARK RYDER 'JOY'

SWING CITY

1995 - PRESENT

UK Garage heavyweight Grant Nelson's label alongside business partner Kate Ross. A home to the many colaborations and solo work by the boss as well as Bump & Flex, Norris 'Da Boss' Windross and many more!

THE ESSENTIALS

N'N'G 'AFUNKINATION'

GROUND 96 'DON'T YOU WANNA?'

THIRST

1998 - 1999

One of Suburban Base's many sub-labels. Releasing a series of ten records from the likes of Ed Case, Paul Benhamin, Carl H, Ray Hurley, Partners in Crime to name a few... The early plates trade for hefty amounts!!

THE ESSENTIALS

PAUL BENJAMIN & CARL H 'DUB PLATE FLAVAS EP'

RAY HURLEY 'BELIEVE IN ME / BE DIRTY'

TIME2FLEX

1997 - 1999

Time 2 Flex stood tall for two years, putting out only 6 releases, but all solid. Featuring tunes by Industry Standard & Deep Impact - these are hard to come by, and require some serious capital to aquire!

THE ESSENTIALS

MAGNETIC FORCE 'THE REFLECTION EP'

DEEP IMPACT 'UNRELEASED PROJECT'

TIME IS NOW

2020 - PRESENT

Promising UK Garage belonging to Shall Not Fade, run out of Bristol, with cuts from the new school's finest, including Yosh, Interplanetary Criminal, Y U QT, Main Phase & so many more...

THE ESSENTIALS

INTERPLANETARY CRIMINAL 'DARKSIDE EP'

HOLLOWAY 'SOME BAD DAYS EP'

UNDA VYBE

1997 - 2000

Karl 'Tuff Enuff' Brown's imprint, fusing the House & Garage sounds of the UK & US,. Tracks from the likes of Kerri Chandler, Matt 'Jam' Lamont, Filthy Rich, Peekay & Zack Toms.

THE ESSENTIALS

BAFFLED & DA STYLUS 'WANNA PLAY'

DAWN TALLMAN 'NEW YORK CITY GIRL (YARDLEY REMIX) '

VERY IMPORTANT PLASTIC

1997 - 2004

Associated with 'London Underground FM', founded by Ramsey & Fen, and most importantly the legendary MJ Cole who had a hand in writing & engineering almost everything on the label.

THE ESSENTIALS

DB SELECTIVE 'DUB TRAIN'

PICES 'NEVER FORGET'

VIBESEY

2020 - PRESENT

Vibesey.

Limited edition vinyl-only label born off the back of a successful UK Garage YouTube channel. So far has releases from Highrise, Masterplan, DJ Para, Perception, Ease Up George & The Thunderkats.

THE ESSENTIALS

DJ PARA 'NINETEEN LONGTIME'
HIGHRISE 'TAKE TIME / UNDERSTAND'

VITAL ESSENCE

1998 - 2000

Established by Teebone - some serious heat on here from the man himself (as Templeton Peck), plus cuts from DJ Stretch, Marc Mac, Dextrous & other Reinforced label artists under their UK Garage aliases!

THE ESSENTIALS

TEMPLETON PECK 'SWEAT'

MAXIMUM STYLE 'WAKE UP'

SOUTHSIDECIRCULARS.COM